To Dove from Yak.
With special thanks to
Esmé, Tara, Jennifer and Scott
(for making this garden grow).

K.M.

To Daniel, the Yak to my Dove.
With a big thank-you to Kyo,
Tara and Charlotte!

E.S.

Tundra Books, an imprint of Penguin Random House Canada Young Readers,
a Penguin Random House Company

LIBRARY AND ARCHIVES CANADA CATALOGUING IN PUBLICATION

Maclear, Kyo, 1970-, author
Yak and dove / Kyo Maclear ; Esmé Shapiro, illustrator.
Issued in print and electronic formats.
ISBN 978-1-77049-494-7 (hardback).—ISBN 978-1-77049-495-4 (EPUB)

I. Shapiro, Esmé, 1992-, illustrator II. Title.
PS8625.L435Y35 2017   jC813'.6   C2016-905921-9   C2016-905922-7

Published simultaneously in the United States of America by Tundra Books of Northern
New York, an imprint of Penguin Random House Canada Young Readers, a Penguin Random
House Company

Library of Congress Control Number: 2016952340

Edited by Tara Walker
Designed by Jennifer Griffiths
The artwork in this book was done with watercolor, gouache and colored pencil,
with help from a few bagels, bowls of borscht and marmalade toast, of course.
The handlettering was rendered by Esmé Shapiro.

Printed and bound in China

www.penguinrandomhouse.ca

1 2 3 4 5   21 20 19 18 17

tundra | Penguin Random House | TUNDRA BOOKS

YAK AND DOVE

words by KYO MACLEAR

pictures by ESMÉ SHAPIRO

tundra

If We Were Twins

Yak?

Yes, Dove.

Do you ever wish we were twins?

No, Dove, I have never
wished that.

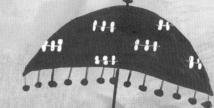

But, Yak, if we were twins,
we could wear matching clothes.

Oh, Dove!
With matching hats
and shoes?

Yes, Yak. And if we were twins,
we could invent rhyming names.

Like Peter and Dieter.

Or Johnny and Ronny.

And if we were twins, Dove,
we would live in the same house.

Yes, Yak. And we would eat
an equal number of cupcakes.

And pour our tea evenly
in our cups.

If we were twins, Yak,
my feet would be cold when
your feet were cold.

And I would smile
when you smile.

Dove? Are twins really like that?

I don't know, Yak. But if we were more alike,
we would . . .

finish each other's sentences.

We would love the same things.

And have the same fears.

But, Yak, we are not alike.

That's true, Dove.
We have never been the same.
Not once.

You are large and I am small.

You have feathers
and I have fur.

You can be a little too quiet.

You can be a little too loud.

And you are smelly, Yak.

And you are ill-mannered, Dove.

You never share your chocolate!

You make fun of my feet!

Well, I think you have terrible taste in music and bowties!

And I find you bossy!

We are clearly not twins, Yak.

Not at all, Dove.

Not even slightly.

I am not smiling at you, Dove.

I am not smiling at you either, Yak.

The Audition

What's wrong, Yak?

Oh, Marmot, I am lamenting.

Why, Yak? Why are you lamenting?

Oh, Marmot! I have lost my best friend.

I'm sorry to hear that, Yak.

What if I never find another?

Don't worry, Yak.
You will find another.

I will?

Yes, I will help you.

First, I will start with a few questions.

Okay.

Yak, what are you looking for in a new best friend?

I am looking for a loyal friend.

Anything else?

Well, Marmot, I am looking for a friend who appreciates fine music.

Is that it?

I would like a friend who values furriness in his companions.

"Values furriness . . ." Got it. Thank you, Yak.

Yak, there are many good ways to find a new best friend.

But, Marmot, what will be *our* way?

Our way will be to hold a talent contest.

But who will enter this contest?
How will you find contestants?

Trust me, Yak. I will find contestants.

Prizes, please.

We are here for the prizes, Marmot.

Thank you for coming.
Please follow me.

I have good news, Yak. I have found your new best friend.

Marmot, may I speak with you for a moment . . . privately?

Of course you may, Yak.

Marmot, I do not think this wolf is my new best friend.

Are you sure, Yak?

I am sure, Marmot. A best friend would not eat me.

Hmm. Yes, I see.

Are there any other contestants?

There is one left, Yak.

DOBEEDOOBEED

OOOOOO!OOO!

Dove?

Yes, Yak?

You sang my
favorite song, Dove.

I did.

And, Dove, you
wore the bowtie
I bought you.

I did.

You do care, Dove.

Yes, Yak, I do.

I'm sorry, Dove.
I can be furry-headed
sometimes.

And I can be flighty
sometimes, Yak.

And I have no self-control.

And I don't like cats.

And yet . . .

And yet.

I would never eat you, Dove. Not in a million years.

I would never eat you either, Yak.

Dove?

Yes, Yak?

Maybe we are a bit alike . . .

after all.

Yak and Quiet

Hello, Yak. What are you doing?

I am making a garden, Dove.

What kind of garden, Yak?

**Shhh, Dove. I am making
a quiet garden.**

RING! RING! **RING!**

Yes. It's Dove. Okay.
Keep all my shares in
futuristic gizmos.
Thank you. Good-bye.

As I was saying, Dove, the world is getting noisier these days.
So I am planting some silence.

That's nice, Yak. Would you like
me to sing to your garden?

No singing, thank you.

RING! RING! RING!

Yes. Dove here. No. Okay. Yes. Okay. Okay. Okay. Okay. Okay. Okay. Okay. Thank you. Good-bye.

Dove, please. I need quiet. Shhhh.

Wait a minute, Yak. What are you doing?
Those are not seeds. Those are marbles.

Well, Dove, a marble is quiet.

But, Yak, a garden
needs proper seeds.

That's your opinion, Dove.

I don't know, Yak.
If you ask me, I don't think
this garden will sprout.

Yak! What are you doing?

I am washing your phone. Look, Dove.
It's so clean now.

Clean? Yak! No!

Please, Dove. I don't need a
noisy friend right now.
What I need is a horticulturist.

Fine. This noisy Dove
is leaving.

RING!
RING!

Hello, Dove. Are you what I think you are?

Yup. I am a horticulturist.

That's great, Dove. Can you help
my plants come up?

Umm . . . yup.

Can you sing my garden a song?

A quiet song, Yak?

Any song.
Oh, Dove,
you were right.
The seeds
were no good.

No, Yak, I was wrong.
There is going to be a garden.

There is? When will it come up?

Shhh, Yak. Have you lost your marbles?
It'll come up when it's ready.

Dove, look! Our singing worked.

So it did.

What should we call our garden, Dove?

We should call it The Very Noisy Quiet Garden.

Very catchy, Dove. I like it.

Thank you, Yak.

You're welcome,
Dove.

What's that in your seed bag, Yak?

Bottle caps. Quiet ones.

Listen, Dove. The frogs are croaking.

Listen, Yak. The owls are hooting.

The world is so noisy.

So very noisy quiet.

Good night, Dove.

Good night, Yak.